This Orchard book belongs to

....

....

For Neha and Suzanna

Thanks to the Home-Start Renfrewshire family group: Julie Alexander, Stephanie Barn,
Joanne Blair, Lynne Ewing, Lyndie Gibson, Mags Gibson, Claire Hamilton, Heather Holton,
Jayne Johnson, Gayle McFedries, Emma McGhee, Dione McGregor, Sumi Mohammed,
Deborah Waite, Audrey Yildirim and Emma Richardson
who collaborated with me on the text for this book.

ORCHARD BOOKS
338 Euston Road, London NW1 3BH
Orchard Books Australia
Level 17/207 Kent Street, Sydney, NSW 2000

First published in 2012 by Orchard Books
First paperback publication in 2012
This edition first published in 2013

ISBN 978 1 40831 632 0

Text and illustrations © Alison Murray 2012

**The right of Alison Murray to be identified as the author and illustrator of this book
has been asserted by her in accordance with the Copyright, Designs and Patents Act, 1988.**

**This book was produced as part of Scottish Book Trust's Early Years
Writer-in-Residence project, in partnership with Home-Start and funded by
the National Lottery through Creative Scotland.**

A CIP catalogue record for this book is available from the British Library.

1 3 5 7 9 10 8 6 4 2

Printed in China

Orchard Books is a division of Hachette Children's Books, an Hachette UK company.
www.hachette.co.uk

www.scottishbooktrust.com
www.home-start.org.uk

Little Mouse

Alison Murray

ORCHARD

Sometimes,
when I'm being very
quiet and cuddly,
my mummy calls me her
little mouse.

But that's
funny because
I'm not little
like a mouse –

I'm tall!

And I am actually very **strong.**

A little mouse nibbles its food
but I chomp like a
hungry horse!

And I'm not timid like a little mouse . . .

I'm **very** brave . . .

...and I can be **scary** too!

grrrr**rrrrr**rr!

I don't really sound like
a little mouse...

Trumpety,
trump,
trump!

Too-wit, tOo-wit,
tOo-woOOo!

yOwly, hOwly,
hOWl!

Squeak!

Oops!
That was a hiccup!

A little mouse
can't fly...

but I can zoom high into the sky!

"Bathtime!"

And I'm pretty certain that little mice don't

stomp . . .

or w^addle...

...or splash!

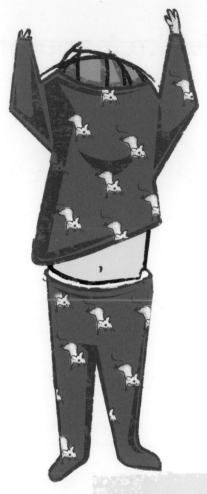

But just now,
right at this very moment,

I think I'm happy to be . . .

...quiet and cosy,

cuddly and dozy...

Mummy's
little
mouse.